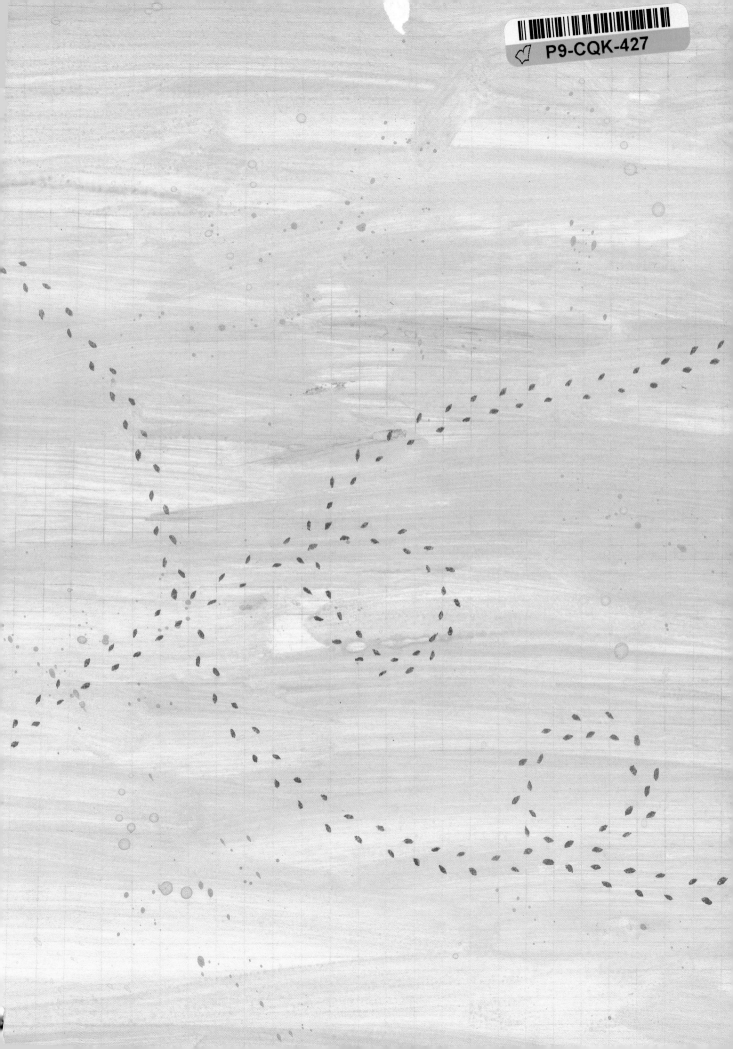

Carin Berger

A
Perfect
Day

Greenwillow Books
An Imprint of HarperCollins*Publishers*

It snowed

and snowed

and snowed

and snowed.

The whole world was white.

_____shire June 16 1863

_____ Richmond Dr
To _____ Salt   50

17

_____ Cole   Dr
To ___ Picketts   8 __

25

John _____   Dr
By 1 days work

E D Cole   Dr
To 112 Picketts   1 44

29

Norman Cotton   Dr
To Cloth from H W Richardson   2 44

July 1
To 1 paper Tobacco   44

6

W P Bennett   Dr
To 774 feet Bass wood boards   2 32

T B Brown   Dr
To sawing 598 feet boards   1 __

Thomas Blin   Dr
To sawing 5146 feet h Samber   13 11
" " " 720 Spruce   2 __
                                      15 27

John Cronon   Dr
To sawing 1598 feet spruce   4 93

Patrick McDonald   Cr
By 4379 feet Log on mountain

Emma got to make the first tracks in the snow . . .

but then Leo whooshed by on his skis.

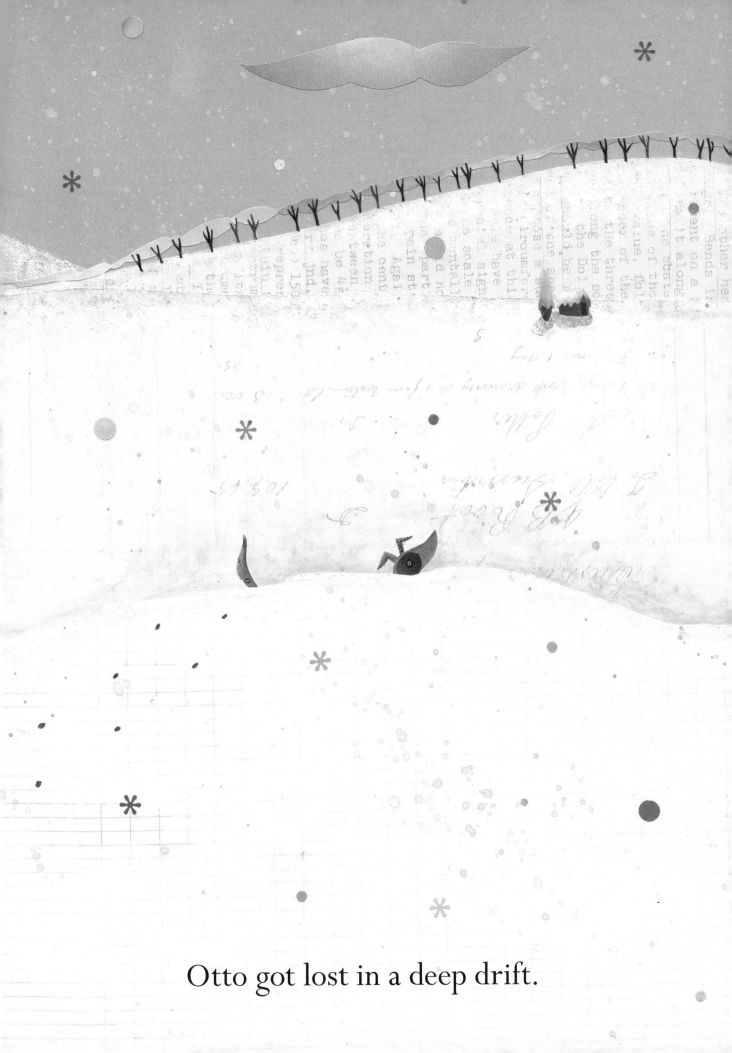

Otto got lost in a deep drift.

Sasha and Max showered Oscar
with a wild flurry of snowballs,

while Willa climbed to the top of a big mountain.

Thea and Lila built the tallest snowman ever.

And the smallest.

Mickey made the *very* best snow fort with Sarah.

Then Everett sped by on a sled.

So did Finn.

And Simone.

And Sophie.

And Sadie.

Nick and Anya spun loop-di-loops

on the frozen pond.

And Charlotte opened an icicle stand.

Then, all together,

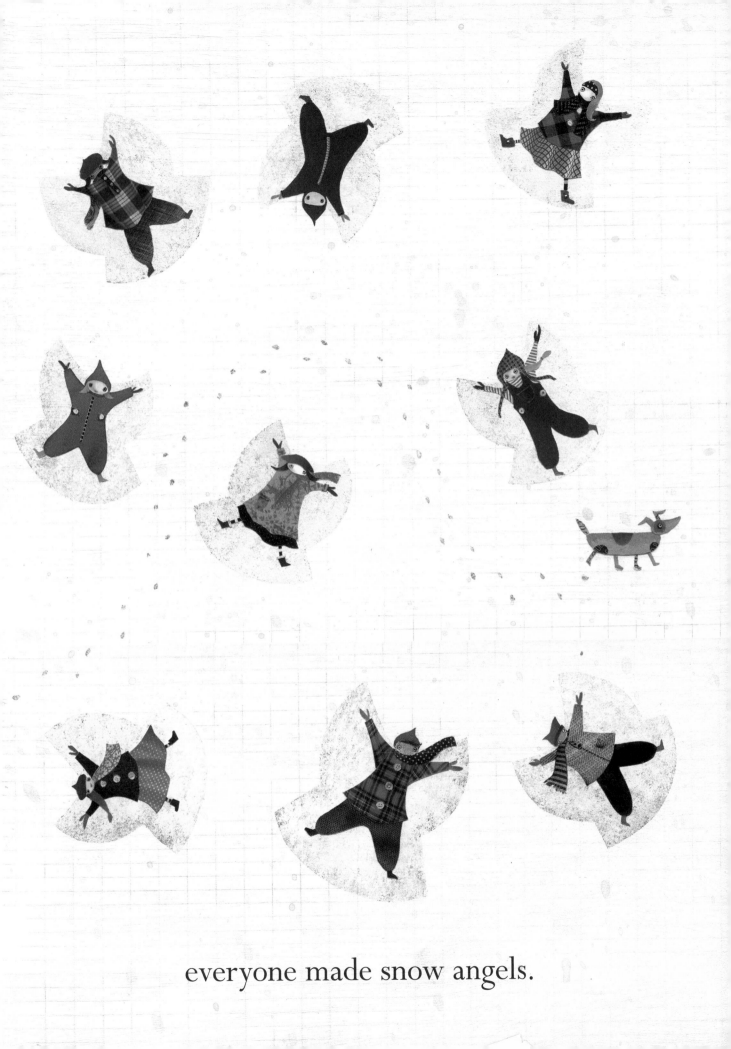

everyone made snow angels.

Dusk came, and the lights blinked on.

It was time to go home to warm hugs

and dry clothes and steaming hot chocolate.

The perfect end to a perfect day.

To my mom, whose deep love of winter is absolutely contagious

A Perfect Day

Copyright © 2012 by Carin Berger

All rights reserved. Manufactured in China.

For information address HarperCollins Children's Books,

a division of HarperCollins Publishers,

10 East 53rd Street, New York, NY 10022.

www.harpercollinschildrens.com

Collages were used to prepare the full-color art.

The text type is 27-point Perpetua.

Library of Congress Cataloging-in-Publication Data

Berger, Carin.

A perfect day / by Carin Berger.

p. cm.

"Greenwillow Books."

Summary: Young friends enjoy a day of sledding, snowball fights,

and ice skating one snowy day in their hillside village.

ISBN 978-0-06-201580-8 (trade ed.)—ISBN 978-0-06-201581-5 (lib. ed.)

[1. Snow—Fiction. 2. Day—Fiction.] I. Title.

PZ7.B45134Per 2012 [E]—dc23 2011035455

12 13 14 15 16 SCP 10 9 8 7 6 5 4 3 2 1

First Edition

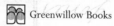 Greenwillow Books

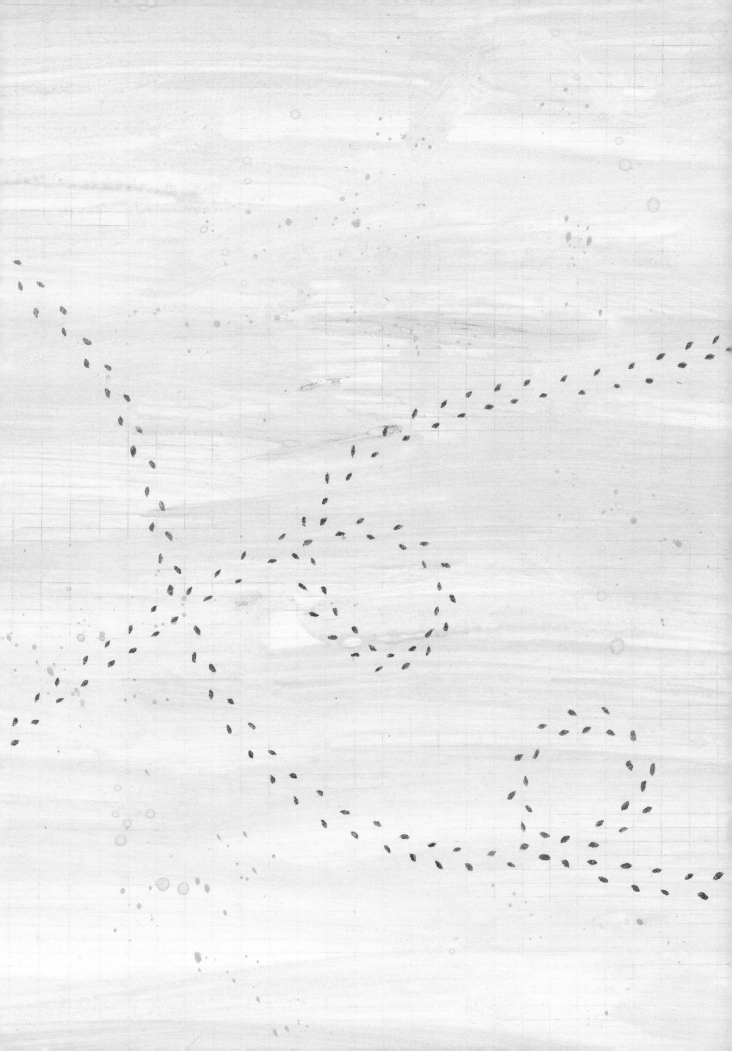

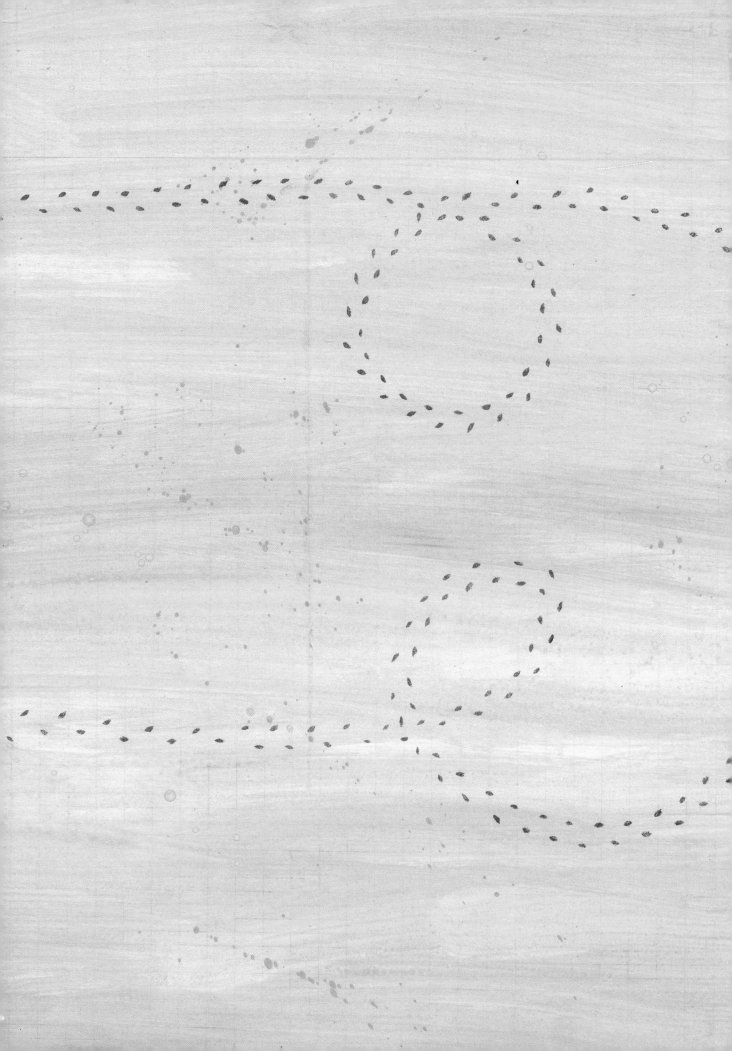